For Louis and Freya
and anyone else who is a bit worried.
J.S.

For every child waiting for a new brother or sister
F.C.

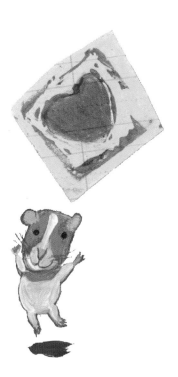

Text copyright © Jonathan Shipton 2009
Illustrations copyright © Francesca Chessa 2009
First published in Great Britain in 2009 by Gullane Children's Books
185 Fleet Street, London EC4A 2HS
First published in the United States of America by Holiday House, Inc. in 2009
All Rights Reserved
Printed and Bound in Indonesia
www.holidayhouse.com
First American Edition
1 3 5 7 9 10 8 6 4 2

Library of Congress Cataloging-in-Publication Data
Shipton, Jonathan.
Baby baby blah blah blah! / by Jonathan Shipton ; illustrated by Francesca Chessa. — 1st American ed.
p. cm.
Summary: When her parents tell her that they are expecting a baby, Emily sets to work on a list of pros and cons.
ISBN 978-0-8234-2213-5 (hardcover)
[1. Babies—Fiction. 2. Lists—Fiction. 3. Family life—Fiction.] I. Chessa, Francesca, ill. II. Title.
PZ7.S5576Bab 2009
[E]—dc22
2008034895

Baby Baby blah blah blah!

by **Jonathan Shipton**

illustrated by

Francesca Chessa

Holiday House / New York

Emily loved to make lists.
She made lists of things she didn't like.
She made lists of things she loved.

One day Emily's mom and dad said,
"Guess what? We're going to have a . . .

... baby!

"Oh," said Emily.
"That's nice."

That night Emily said, "You know this baby, is it going to be a brother or a sister?"
"It's going to be a surprise," said Emily's dad.
Emily's mom patted her round baby bump.

Well, the baby bump grew. And a little worry started to grow
in Emily's mind. And the bigger the baby bump grew,
the bigger Emily's worry grew.

"That's it!"
she shouted.
"I've had enough."
And she zoomed off.

A little while later, Emily came into the kitchen.
"Guess what I've been doing," she said.
"Have you been making a list?" asked Emily's dad.
"Yes, I have," admitted Emily.
"Good," said Emily's dad.
"It's not that good," warned Emily.

A baby is good because...

It is
really tiny.

Its head is soft and snuffly.

You can play pat-a-cake.

When it has grown a little
you can feed it all kinds
of mushy baby food.

You can take it out
for rides in the
stroller.

You can swoosh it
through puddles.

You can tickle it to bits!

"Well done!" said Emily's mom.
"Yes, BUT. . . ," continued Emily darkly,
"you haven't heard the other part."

cry.

WAAA!

It cries if it's hungry.

It cries if it's thirsty.

It cries if it's tired.

It cries if it's hot.

It cries if it wants to poop.

"But that's not the worst thing," said Emily. "When the baby comes . . .

". . . it will be baby this and baby that
and baby goo goo and baby blah blah blah.
Everything will be upside down
and inside out."

"But it's not going to be like that," said Emily's dad. "Come and sit on my lap and I will tell you a story about a baby."
"See!" said Emily triumphantly. "It's already started!

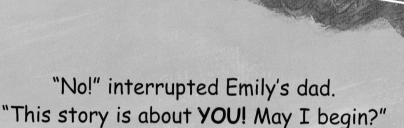
Baby baby blah blah blah!"

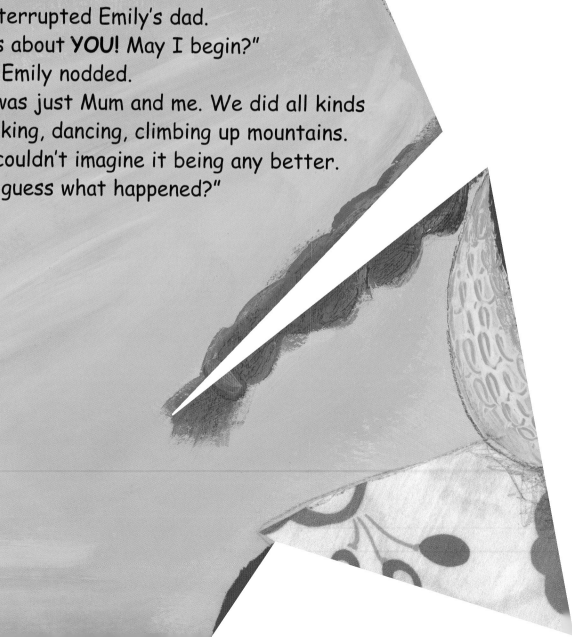

"No!" interrupted Emily's dad.
"This story is about **YOU!** May I begin?"
Emily nodded.
"A long time ago there was just Mum and me. We did all kinds of stuff together: walking, dancing, climbing up mountains. We were so happy I couldn't imagine it being any better. But then guess what happened?"

"Me . . . ?" said Emily.
"Yes! But having you didn't stop us;
we just took you along too!"
"Even up mountains?" said Emily suspiciously.
Emily's dad smiled.
"Well, maybe not up mountains. . . ."

"But we did go on bike rides together,"
said Emily's mom.
"And now we go skating together," said Emily.
"Exactly! It just gets better and better, doesn't it?"
Emily's dad asked.
"Maybe," agreed Emily.

"And . . . ," continued Emily's mom, "we will always make time for hugs and laps and stories. Because we will

always love you!

No matter what the babies do."

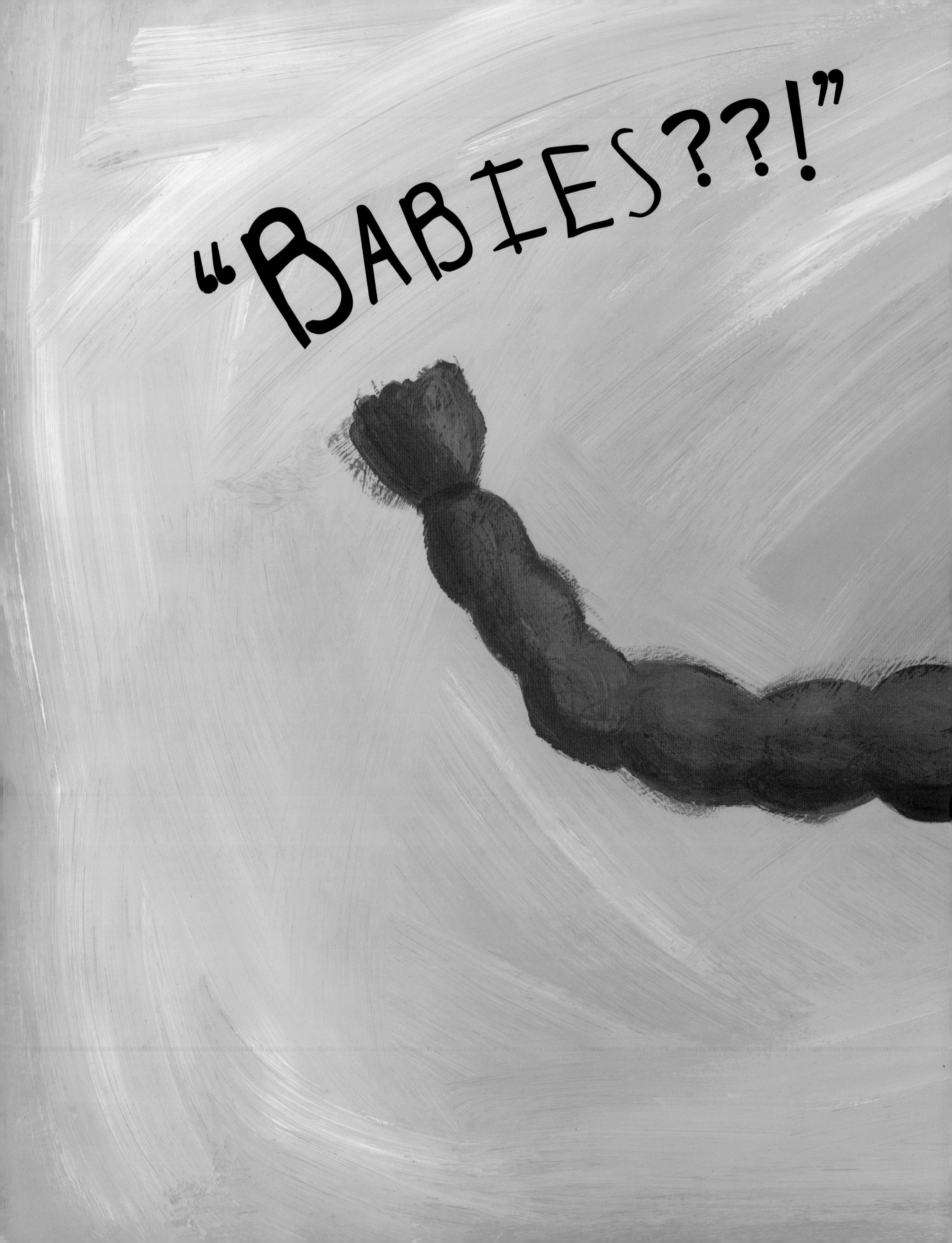
"BABIES??!"